Written by Cindy Kenney

Illustrated by Dennis Bredow

Based on the video: *The Star of Christmas*

Created by Phil Vischer and Tim Hodge

BIG IDEA BOOKS™

Zonderkidz

For my family – Jim, Andy, and Jimmy
Who add to the joy of Christmas
more than they know

www.bigidea.com

Zonder**kidz**™
The children's group of Zondervan
www.zonderkidz.com

The Star of Christmas
Copyright © 2002 by Big Idea Productions, Inc.

Requests for information should be addressed to:
Zonderkidz, Grand Rapids, Michigan 49530

ISBN: 0-310-70504-5

Written by: Cindy Kenney
Editors: Cindy Kenney and Gwen Ellis
Cover and Interior Illustrations: Dennis Bredow
Cover Design and Art Direction: John Trent
Interior design: Karen Poth

Library of Congress applied for

Printed in United States
02 03 04 05/PC/5 4 3 2 1

Seymour Schwenk zoomed through the streets of London. His rocket engine backfired as he zipped along. People stared. Horses neighed. Seymour was causing quite a ruckus! London in 1880 had never seen anything like it.

As he pulled up in front of the theater and hopped out of his peculiar contraption, he was met by Millward Phelps and Cavis Appythart. They were very anxious to meet him.

Millward admired Seymour's rocket-powered invention as Cavis talked about their upcoming production of *The Princess and the Plumber,* a musical spectacular scheduled to open in just three days, on Christmas Eve.

Spying the package that Seymour was carrying, Millward asked, "Cavis what's in the box?"

"Well, in this modern age, it isn't enough to just have a great story," Cavis explained. "No! You need to show the audience something they've never seen before!"

"You've got a monkey that can yodel?" Millward asked.

"No, Millward. *Electric lights!* Spectacle's the name of the game!" Cavis explained.

But Cavis knew it wouldn't be enough to just have spectacular lights for the big show. He knew that any show worth seeing in London was attended by Prince Frederick. Not only was Frederick heir to the throne, but he was also London's number-one theater critic! A good word from him and the show was sure to be a success.

Cavis and Millward stood back to stare up at the marquee of the theater. They were mesmerized by the bigness of what they were about to do— tell London a wonderful story about a sad princess and a kindly plumber and the power of love!

"Wow!" Cavis said as he backed right into a lamppost with a poster advertising *another* Christmas program. This other program was going to be held at Saint Bart's, a local church. It was a new Christmas production at Saint Bart's, and it was also going to be performed on Christmas Eve.

"I'm going over to Saint Bart's and see what's going on," said Cavis as he hurried off.

avis stood in the back of St. Barts and watched as six-year-old Edmund Gilbert was busy getting ready for that Christmas pageant. Reverend Gilbert, Edmund's dad, also watched as his son barked out orders and tried to corral all the manpower he could to make his production bigger and better than ever! But his dad explained that the show didn't have to be a huge spectacle, because the story of Christmas is so simple and powerful all by itself. But Edmund wasn't so sure. He had twenty pounds of glitter to make *sure* his message shone through.

When Edmund's dad explained that there was a family across town who needed help, Edmund was quite disappointed that his dad couldn't stay around to help with the pageant.

"Helping people in need is more important, Edmund. That's what God did on Christmas. He came to Earth to help us and to show *us* how much he loved us. 'She will give birth to a son…and they will call him Immanuel—God with us,'" his dad explained. "I need to help this family first; then I'll be back."

"Oh! By the way, the church committee decided that you can use the Star of Christmas in your program if you're very careful with it," Reverend Gilbert added as he turned to leave. "You'll find it in the cabinet by the communion supplies."

Cavis laughed; he'd seen enough. "It's just a bunch of kids, puttin' on a church play! Don't know why I was so worried," he muttered as he turned to leave. "But I do wonder what the 'Star of Christmas' is!"

avis didn't have to wonder for long. The next day the *London Post Gazette* read: "Saint Gregory the Great gave the Star to the monks at Canterbury on August 14, 592. It is a very *special* star, and it hasn't been publicly displayed for years."

"Wow! We should go!" Millward said when he and Cavis saw the story on the front page of the *Gazette.* This was *big* news. He had forgotten all about their own show.

Cavis tried not to worry. After all, the prince was still coming to their show. And any show worth seeing in London simply had to have Prince Frederick in attendance.

But just then the phone rang. It was the prince informing Cavis and Millward that he would no longer be attending *The Princess and the Plumber* because he was going to see the star.

Cavis began to panic. "We need a lot more lights!" he declared. But then he got another idea…

**A**fter Reverend Gilbert left the church and the church caretaker went to bed, a red shape slowly rose up between two pews and whispered, "Okay, Millward. I think it's clear!"

"I don't feel very good about stealing the star," Millward mumbled as they made their way over to the cabinet where the star had been stored.

"Oh no! We're not *stealing* the star. We're just *borrowing* it," Cavis said. "Besides, we're doing this for London! They're practically *begging* us to borrow it."

"I don't hear them," Millward said as he looked around to see if someone was talking.

"M-metaphorically speaking," Cavis said, nervously.

They carefully pulled a case out of the cabinet that held the star and gazed inside. "It looks like a… turtle," Millward said.

"Well, yes, I suppose…if you look at it that way. But back then, I'm sure it was quite exquisite!" Cavis answered.

"It looks like a turtle," he said, trying to look at it from a different angle.

"I don't care if it looks like a chicken on a bicycle! *This* is what the prince wants to see, so *this* is what we're putting in our show!" Cavis whispered as he helped Millward slip it into his bag.

Silently they crept back toward the door. Then it happened. "Crash!" The cloth holding the fancy communion plates caught on the bag they were carrying. The communion plates clattered onto the stone floor and wobbled about. Cavis and Millward jumped.

"Who's there?" came a voice from the back of the church building.

"Let's get out of here!" Cavis and Millward shouted to one another as they ran for the door.

When Cavis and Millward discovered the back doors of the church were locked, they made a mad dash up the stairs. They hurried through an area covered with scaffolds, ladders, and winches being used to refurbish the bell tower.

"You're gonna be singing out the other side of yer nose when I'm through with you, you slimy sea-donkeys!" the caretaker bellowed after them.

As they reached the landing, Cavis spotted a wooden platform hanging from a rope attached to a pulley hanging from the tower. This must be an elevator, Cavis thought as he hopped up onto the platform. But the block of wood that kept the platform from falling popped loose and the rope began to spin! Cavis plunged down the tower, screaming for help.

A red blur whooshed by the caretaker, causing him to do a double take, spin around, and head back down the stairs. "You can't get away from me, wee tomato! I'll chase ya all the way ta Yorkshire, if I have to!"

Cavis hit bottom with a loud "bang." A big cloud of dust billowed up around him.

re you okay, Cavis?" Millward called, leaning over the railing. But Millward leaned so far over the rail that he knocked a board out from under a shelf holding three huge bells! Millward ducked as the bells whizzed by his head and landed heavily in a basket tied to the other end of Cavis' rope!

Now the heavy basket plunged down the tower, pulling Cavis skyward with incredible speed! Once again, the caretaker caught sight of a red blur going up as he hurried down the stairs.

That's the last straw, yo-yo tomato!" he called after Cavis.

At the top, Cavis jumped off the platform and landed right next to Millward.

"Cavis! Are you okay? You fell down! And then you fell up! Speak to me!" Millward wailed.

Cavis was amazingly unhurt! He quickly shook off his wooziness as he and Millward headed toward a ladder propped up against a wall. They scrambled up the ladder with the caretaker close behind.

"Don't even think you can get away! Yer trapped like a bug on the queen's sticky buns!" he called after them. "Yer trapped like me mother's meatloaf at a church picnic!"

As Millward leaned back to look at the caretaker, the ladder began tipping away from the wall.

The caretaker's eyes followed their flight backward from the wall and right out the window of the bell tower!

"Aaaaaaaaaahhhhhhhh!" Cavis and Millward screamed.

With a loud "thud," Cavis and Millward landed in a laundry cart resting at the bottom of the tower walls. As they lay beneath the laundry, catching their breath, the cart began rolling down a steep, winding hill.

"Are we moving?" Cavis asked as the speeding cart disappeared around a curve in the road.

His question was answered with a thunderous "crash!"

The next day, the cast of *The Princess and the Plumber* stared at Millward and Cavis as they entered the theater. They were bandaged and bruised.

"Okay, everybody!" Cavis called out, pretending not to notice that everyone was staring at them. "I want to see the final dress rehearsal of the spectacular closing number with lights and the 'you-know-what'!"

Everyone scurried into position as the music began. Slowly, and quite dramatically, the Faerie Peas were lowered on tiny swings covered with little lightbulbs.

"With her crown and with his wrench… he a Brit, and she so French! Nevermore to smell the stench of plugged-up love!" they sang, as Cavis watched excitedly. "They will come from near and far to see a love shine like a star!"

The cast members gazed in delight as Seymour grabbed a rope and the star was lowered. Millward still thought it looked a lot like a turtle.

"Okay! Time for the lights!" Cavis beamed.

Seymour threw switches, and the entire stage came alive with light!

Then, with a final tug, Seymour threw the last switch. This time, there was a loud "pop," followed by several smaller pops. The lights flickered. Everyone glanced nervously around. Seymour looked on in horror as two wires shorted out, starting a fire that quickly spread to the theater's curtain!

With lightning speed, the flames spread. Cast members shrieked and ran as Cavis cried out, "The star!" being forced to leave without it.

The fire spread so quickly that the entire stage was soon engulfed in flames.

Cavis and Millward sat on the sidewalk in front of the burned-out theater, looking forlorn. "The show's gone. The star's gone. The theater's gone. I guess things can't get any worse," Cavis mumbled miserably.

ust then they heard, "It's them, Constable! The vicious hooligans that stole the Star of Christmas!"

Before they knew what had happened, Cavis and Millward heard the cell doors being slammed shut with a noisy "clang."

"Christmas Eve in jail! *That* wasn't part of the plan," Cavis moaned. "I just wanted to teach London to love!"

Cavis and Millward continued to comfort each other as Charles Pincher, a tough-looking con man, emerged from the shadows of their cell.

"Teach London to love?" Charles asked. "Now how exactly were you gonna do that?"

Cavis hopped off his bunk and over to the bars. "With a big stage show with great songs and costumes. And *lots* of lights!"

Charles leaned back into the shadows and began to laugh. "Teach London to love with lightbulbs? You're more likely to teach a horse to fly than to teach *this* city to love—or any city, for that matter!"

"Hasn't anyone ever been nice to you?" Cavis asked.

"Oh sure. Any bloke'll be nice to ya when 'e *wants* somethin' from ya. But that ain't love. Helpin' someone who needs help… when ya won't get nothin' back. Now *that's* love!" Charles told them. "But I ain't ever seen anything like that. Leastwise not 'round 'ere. Teach London to love with lightbulbs! That's a good one!" he chuckled mockingly.

avis and Millward were thoroughly depressed. But then a door opened and, much to their surprise, in walked Reverend Gilbert and his son, Edmund.

"I guess you're pretty mad about the star, huh?" Cavis groaned. "Well, go ahead. Yell away! We're getting what we deserve."

"We aren't here to yell at you," the reverend explained. "Actually, it was Edmund's idea to come. I've been teaching him about Christmas—that God loved us so much he sent his Son, Jesus. And Jesus came to help us, even when we didn't deserve it, just because he loved us!"

Cavis and Millward looked at each other. They didn't understand *what* was happening.

"We wanted to do the same thing for *you*. We aren't gonna press charges!" Edmund beamed.

The faces of Cavis and Millward slowly lit up as the doors of the police station burst open and they were set free to walk back out into the streets of London. But back in his cell, Charles Pincher groaned. *He* was just plain confused.

"Well, since we don't have anything else to do, we can come see your pageant!" Cavis told them.

That's when the reverend explained that they couldn't possibly get there in time for the show. The reverend and Edmund had given up the pageant just to help Cavis and Millward, so they wouldn't have to spend Christmas in jail.

Then a familiar clanking sound distracted them. Seymour drove up in his rocket carriage and Millward had an idea!

Since there weren't any other options, Seymour agreed to let them borrow his contraption to get them to the church on time!

"Let me get this straight," Millward said, hurriedly reviewing Seymour's directions. "Rockets one to four have been used up. Five to ten have to get us there. And under no circumstances are we to use rocket eleven because it hasn't been tested. Okay! Hang on everybody!"

Millward fired up rocket five, and with him fumbling with the steering control, they zoomed down the street, scattering people.

"You don't know how to steer it?" Cavis asked, his eyes opened wide with fear.

"I forgot to ask!" Millward howled.

Hurtling forward out of control, they crashed through a wagon filled with ladies' hats. Then they plowed through a bakery and came out the other end, adorned with various pastries.

"Millward! The bank!" Cavis yelled as they smashed through the front door. The carriage zoomed out the back with the passengers now sporting bankers' hats. Then they were shocked to see a real, live banker seated beside them!

veryone cheered as they zipped down the last street toward the drawbridge that crossed the Thames River. But the last rocket fizzled and died just as the drawbridge began to rise.

"We're not *completely* out of rockets," Millward told them as his eyes lingered on the lever marked Number Eleven. "The show must go on!" he shouted as he fired the forbidden rocket.

The back of the carriage began to rumble. The terrified passengers shook like a group of astronauts in a rocket on a launchpad. Then suddenly, "Vrrrrroooooom"! The carriage took off like a… well, like a rocket! It flew off the bridge and streaked down the street at the height of the rooftops!

Guests were arriving for the pageant as the carriage descended and bounced loudly through the streets near the church's property. Blurs of color whizzed by the prince as the veggies flew down the aisle and landed at the front of the church sanctuary.

Thinking that the show had begun, the audience began to applaud.

But you don't have the Star of Christmas!" Cavis whispered to Edmund as he stood to start the show.

"Sure we do," Edmund answered. "You didn't steal the real Star of Christmas. That's not something you can steal. In fact, it isn't some*thing* at all! It's Someone, Someone very special!"

Everyone turned to look at the small manger on the stage. Cavis and Millward smiled as they realized Edmund was talking about Jesus, the true Star of Christmas.

an you guys help me out?" Edmund asked Cavis and Millward. "I do need a new star of Bethlehem.

"Yeah, we can handle that!" Cavis answered as they hurried offstage.

The pageant began as Edmund narrated, and the audience hung on very word.

"She wrapped him in cloths and placed him in a manger, because there was no room for them in the inn. And an angel of the Lord appeared to shepherds living out in the fields. They said, 'Do not be afraid. I bring you good news of great joy that will be for all people. Today, in the town of David, a Savior has been born to you; he is Christ the Lord!'"

Backstage, Cavis snapped into action. The sound of a squeaky pulley echoed through the church as Millward appeared onstage. Wearing a heavily-glittered star costume, he rose up from behind the manger scene, pulled skyward by the same pulley used in the bell tower.

"And all this took place to fulfill what the prophet had said: 'She will give birth to a son, and they will call him Immanuel—God with us,'" Edmund read on. The music swelled, and the audience roared with approval and applause.

"Hmm. I think I understand!" Cavis exclaimed to Reverend Gilbert, who was standing beside him. "There's only one story that can *really* show us how to love… and this is it!"

As soon as you understand what God did for us at that first Christmas—and how much he loves us—it makes you want to share that love with everyone!" the reverend explained.

"We did it!" Cavis said, gleefully. "We brought love to London on Christmas!"

The cast gathered together to take a bow as Edmund called backstage for Cavis to join them. Forgetting about his role as Millward's counterweight, Cavis eagerly hopped off his platform, causing his board to quickly rise.

"Aaaaahhhhhh!" Millward hollered as he fell with a loud "crash."

The audience gasped.

"I'm okay!" Millward called to the greatly relieved audience, who resumed their ovation.

After the show, the caretaker came down the aisle, yelling, "Hold on a second! Look what I found!" Cavis and Millward held their breath as he carefully opened a square box that revealed the beautiful Star of Christmas.

"It was in me sock drawer all along! I set out the wrong box," he told a delighted crowd who had gathered to see the star.

"If that's the star, what did *we* take?" Cavis asked.

"Our *other* famous relic, the 'Turtle of Damascus'!" he chuckled. "Not nearly as valuable. In fact, most experts say it's a hoax."

"I thought it looked like a turtle," said Millward.

Back at the police station, the jail door leading to Charles Pincher's cell creaked open. Charlie's eyes widened as Cavis and Millward hopped toward his cell, carrying brightly-wrapped packages, food, and colorful Christmas decorations. Charlie didn't know what to say. Was all this for him?

Soon his dark cell was transformed into a festive Christmas party. As the presents and food were brought out, Charlie's cold, hard face melted slowly into a warm one with a big smile.

From out on the street, the little jail cell glowed with enough love, it seemed, to light all of London.

"Merry Christmas, Mr. Pincher," Cavis said, smiling warmly.

Merry Christmas, indeed!